Copyright © 2011, 2012 by Lemniscaat, Rotterdam, The Netherlands

First published in The Netherlands under the title *Vrolijk*

Text & illustration copyright © 2011 by Mies van Hout

English translation copyright © 2012 by Lemniscaat USA LLC • New York

All rights reserved.

AFirst published in the United States and Canada in 2012 by Lemniscaat USA LLC • New York

Distributed in the United States by Lemniscaat USA LLC • New York

Library of Congress Cataloging-in-Publication Data is available.

ISBN 13: 978-1-935954-14-9 (Hardcover)

Printing and binding: Worzalla, Stevens Point, WI USA

First U.S. edition

Happy

MIES VAN HOUT

LEMNISCAAT 8 NEW YORK

curious

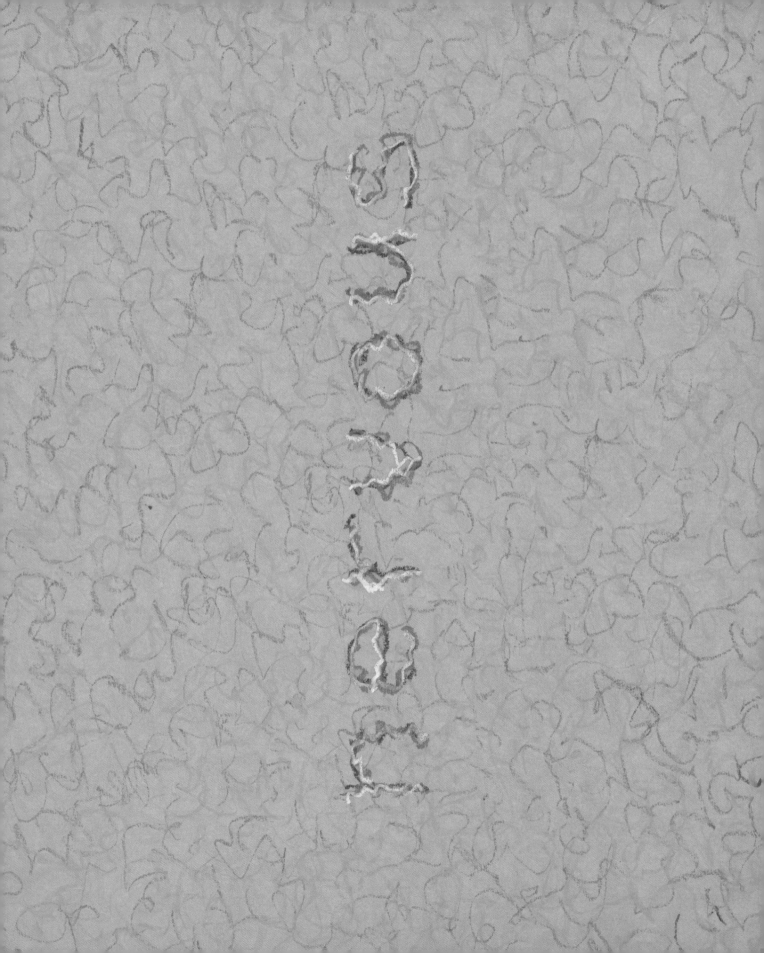

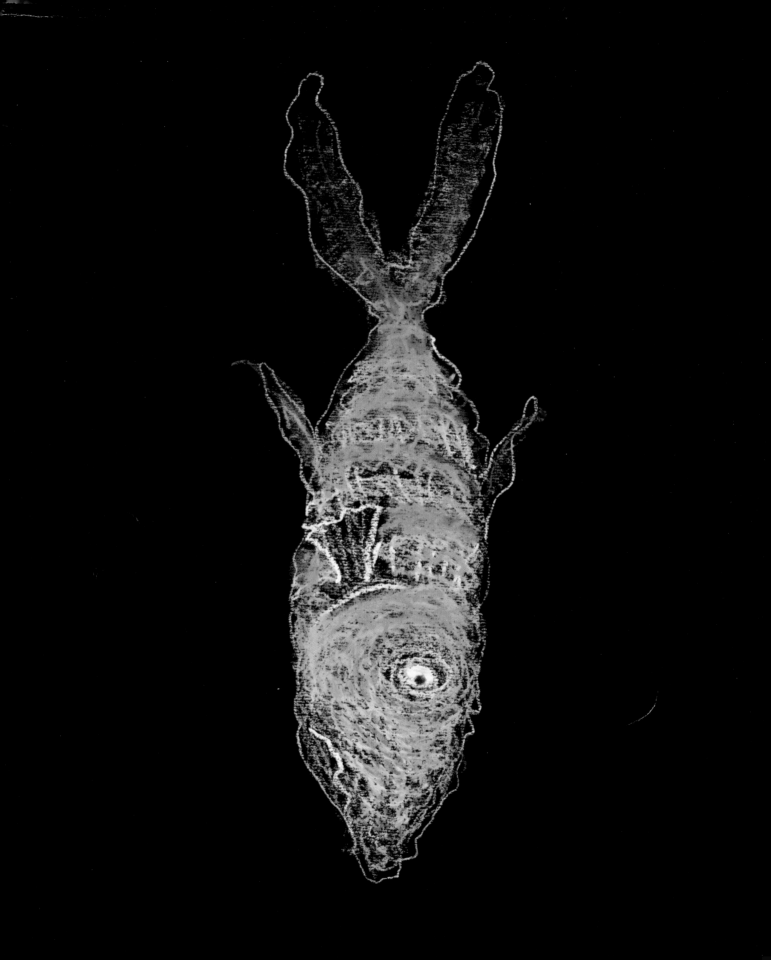

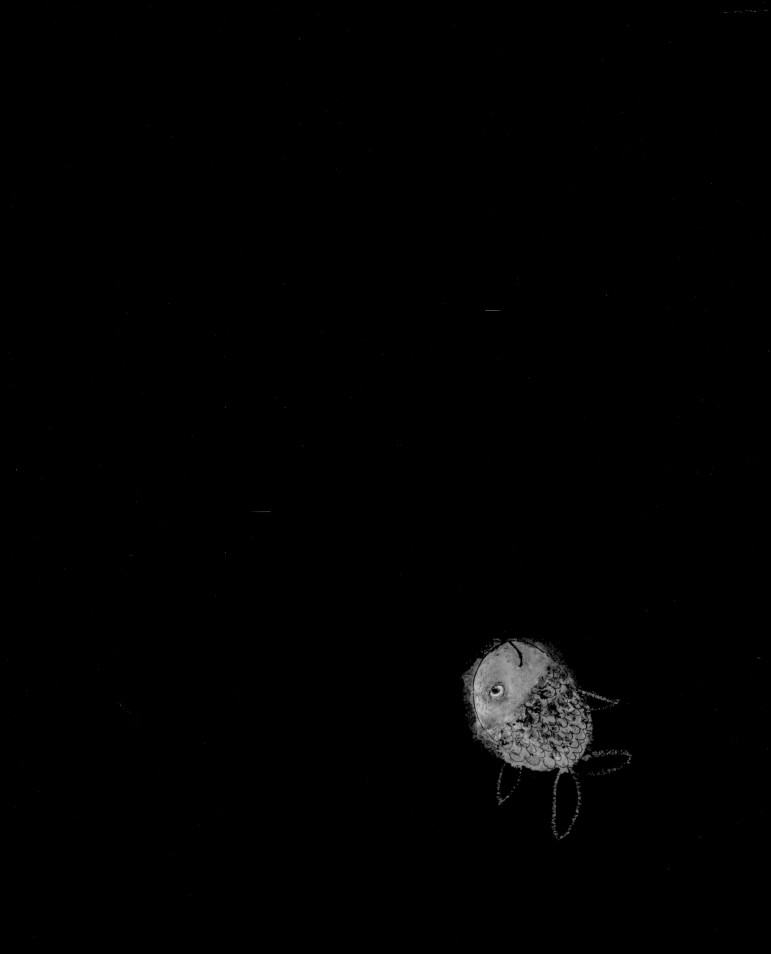

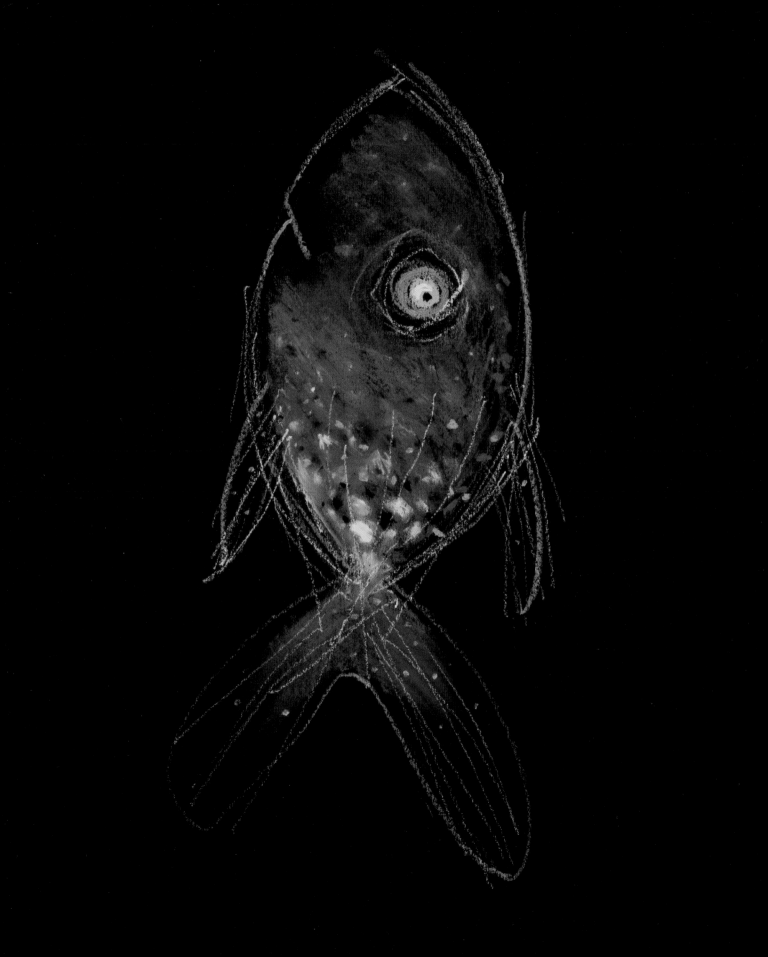

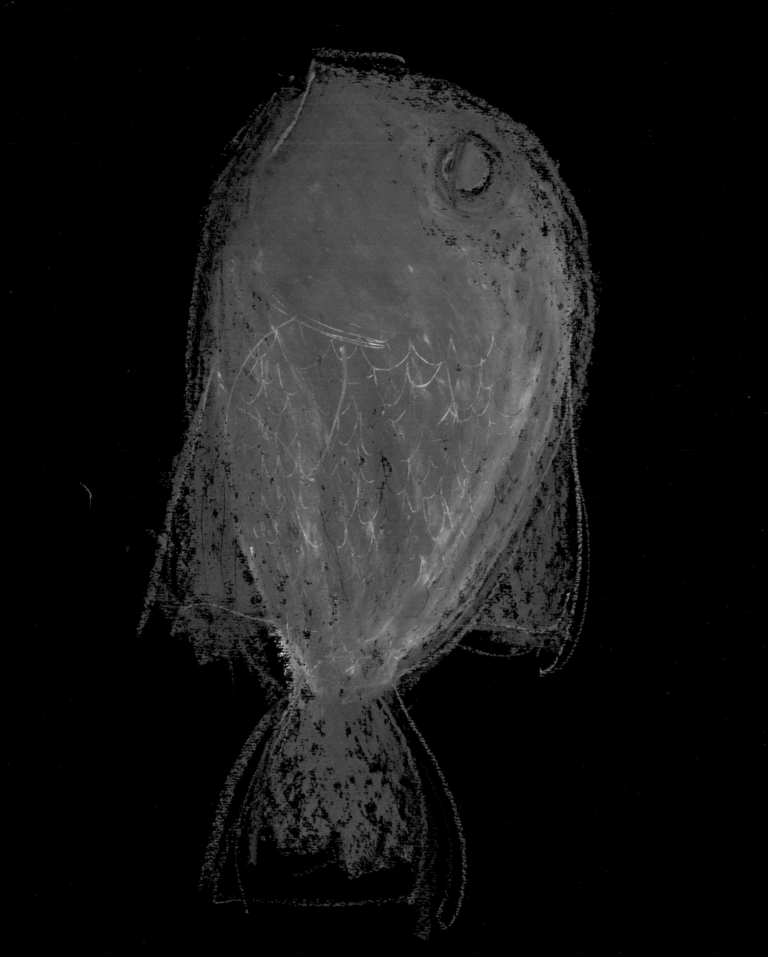

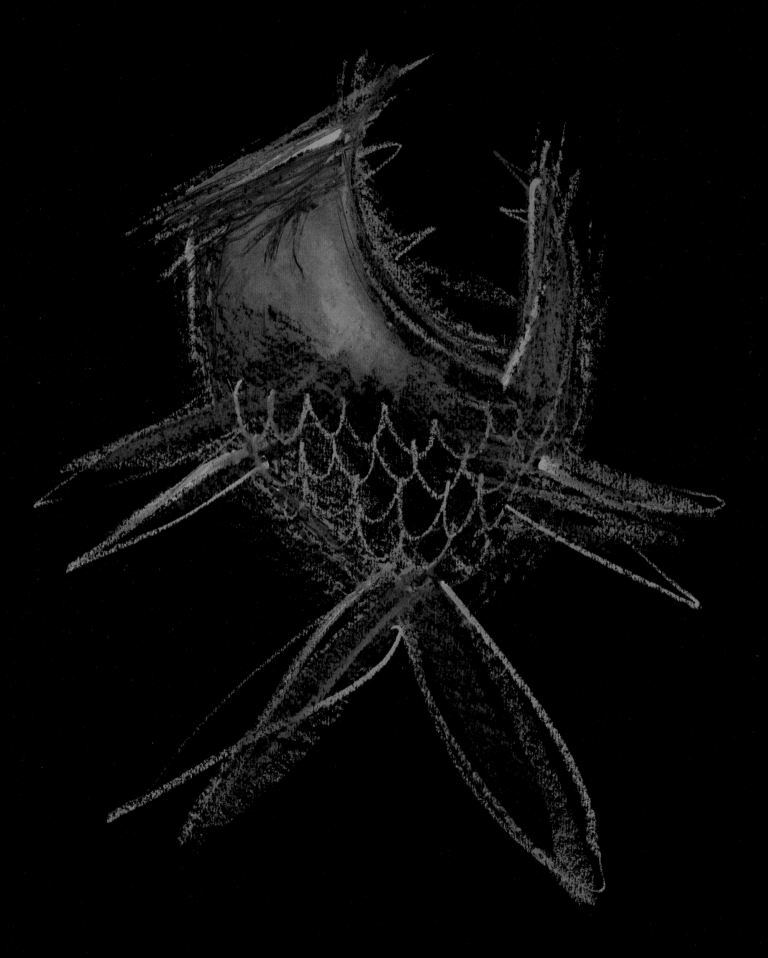

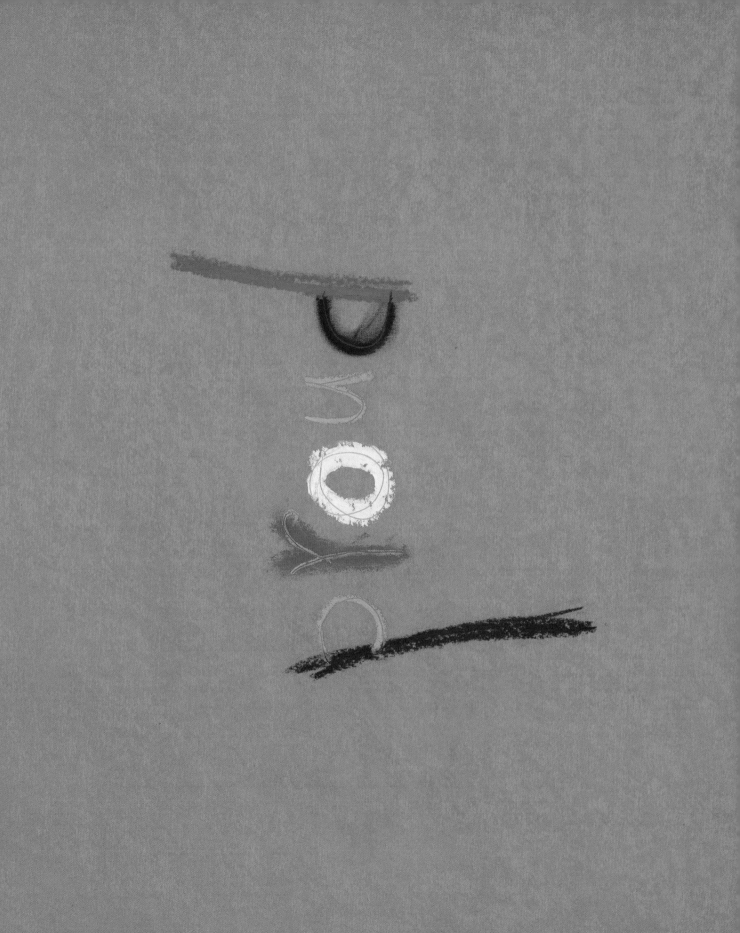

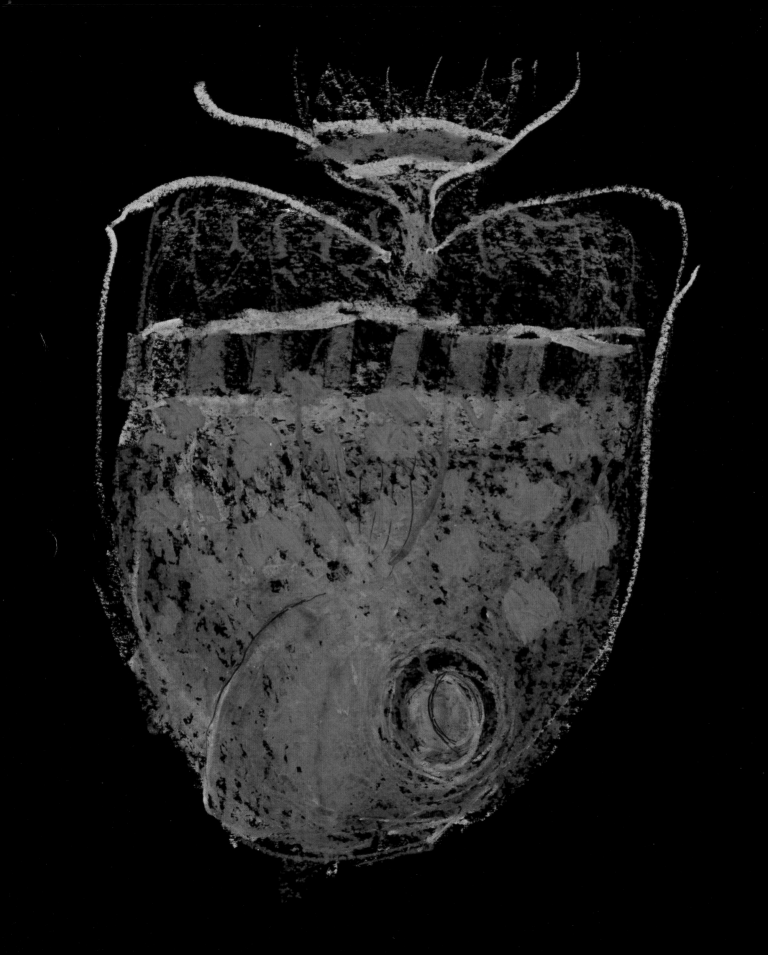

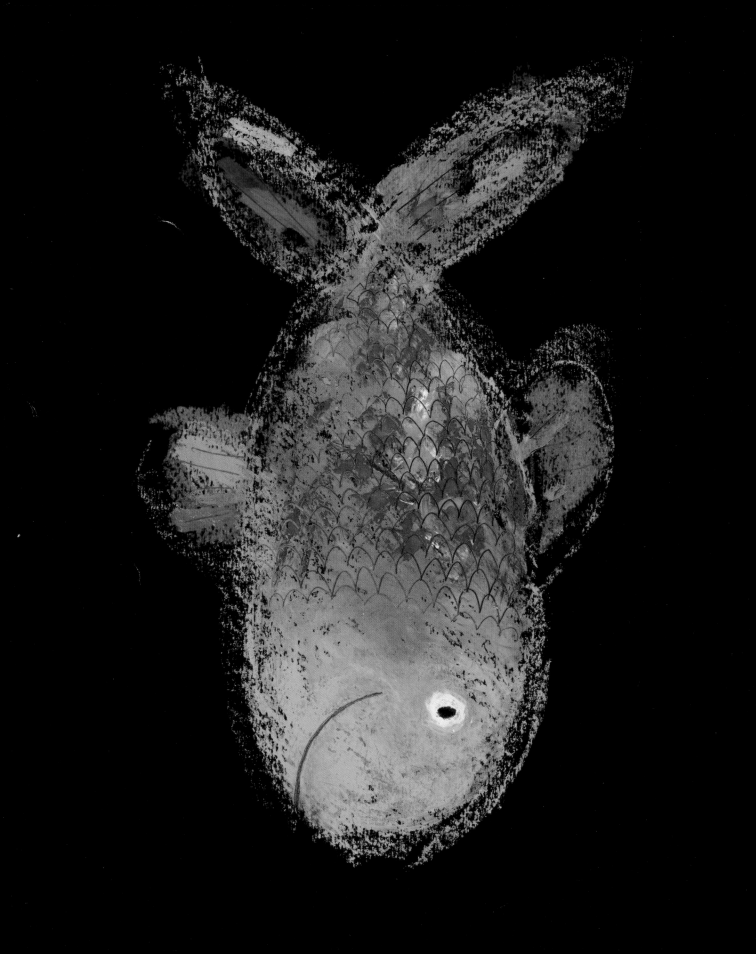

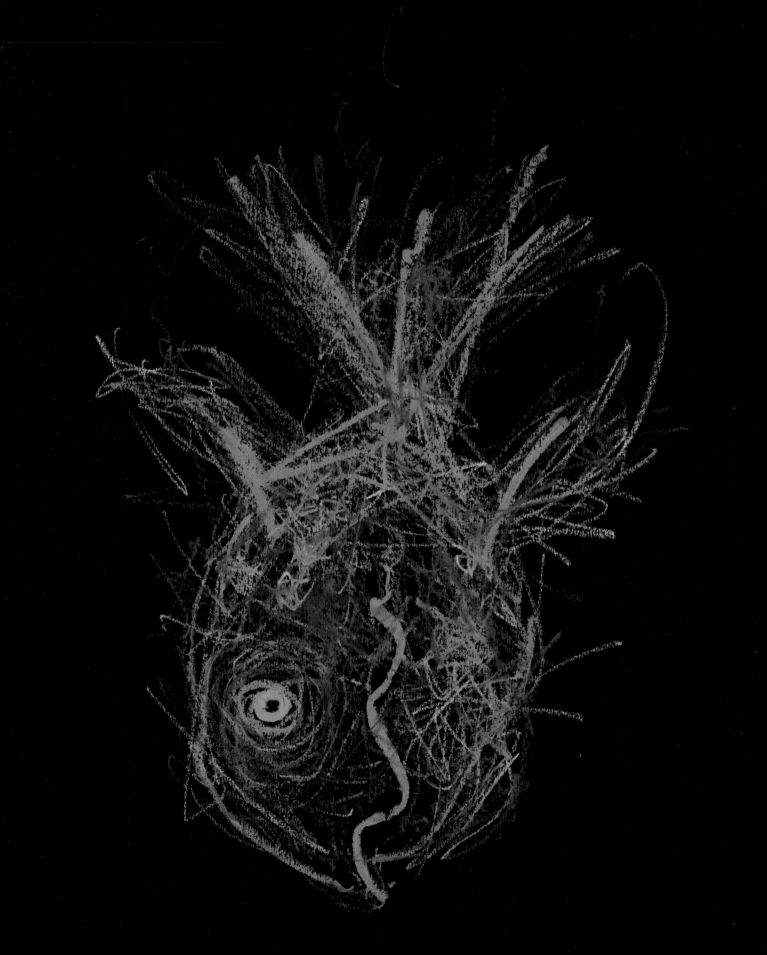

content

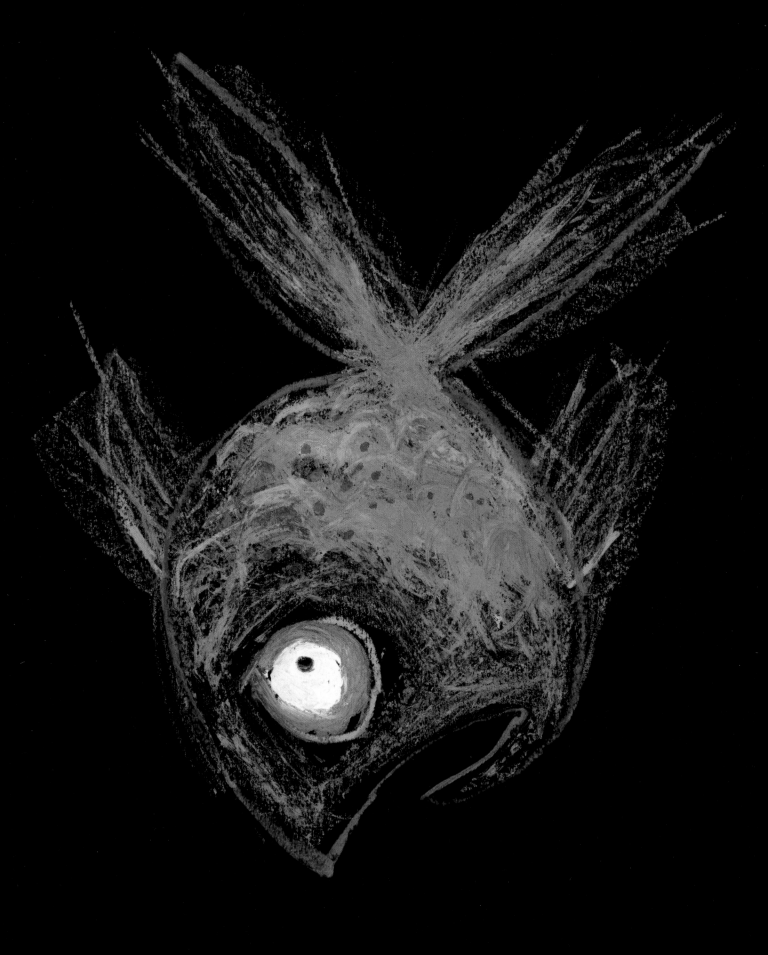

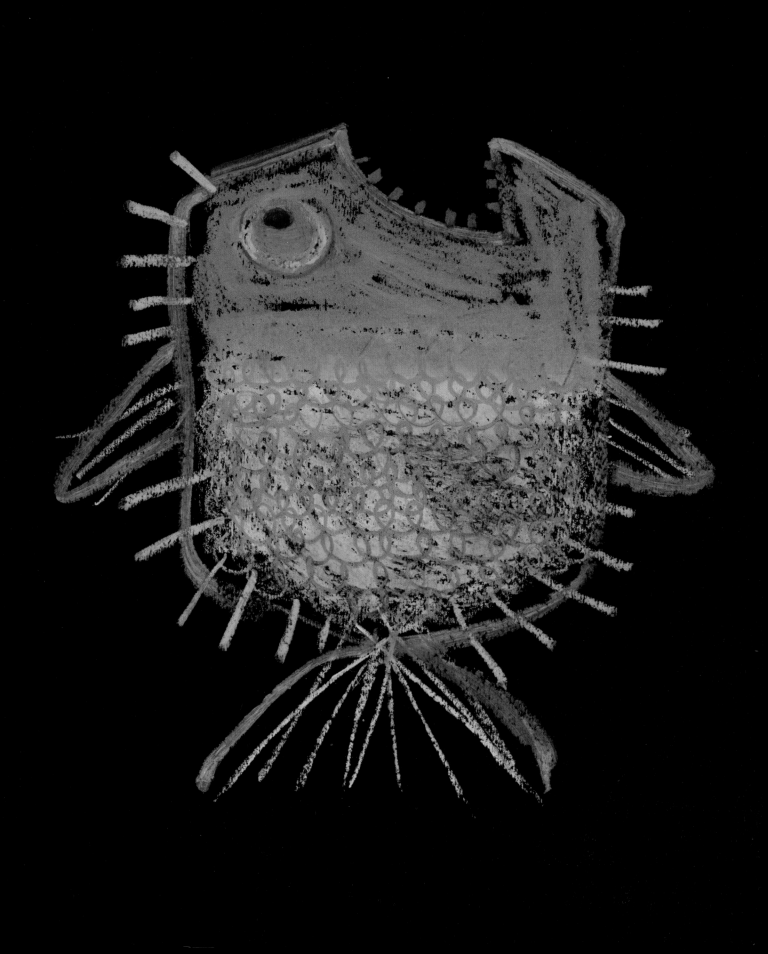

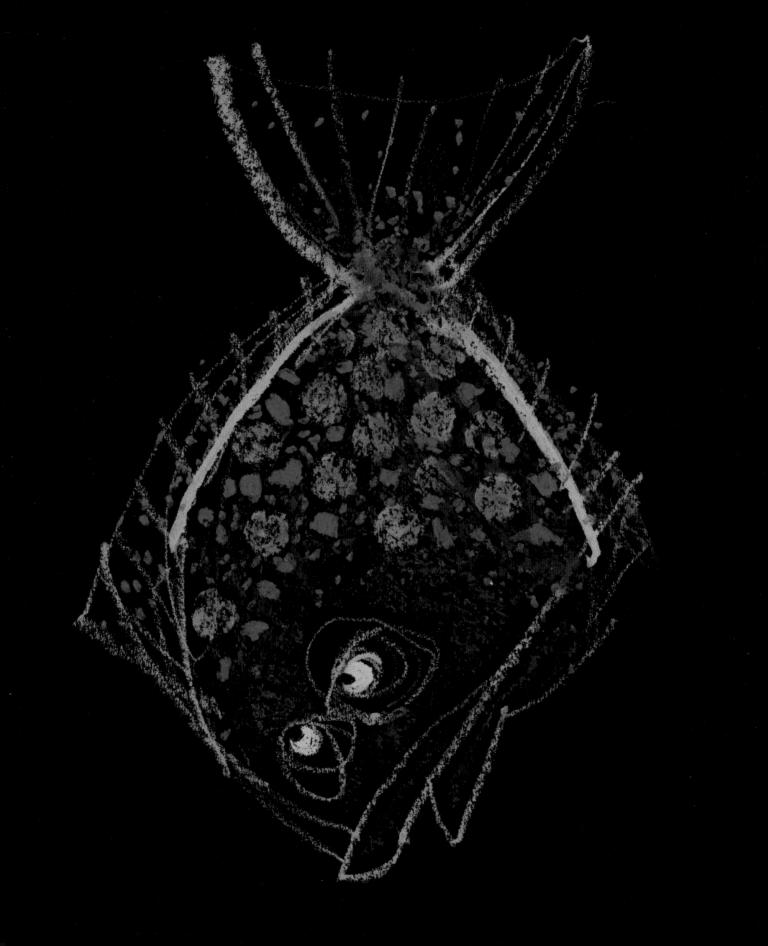

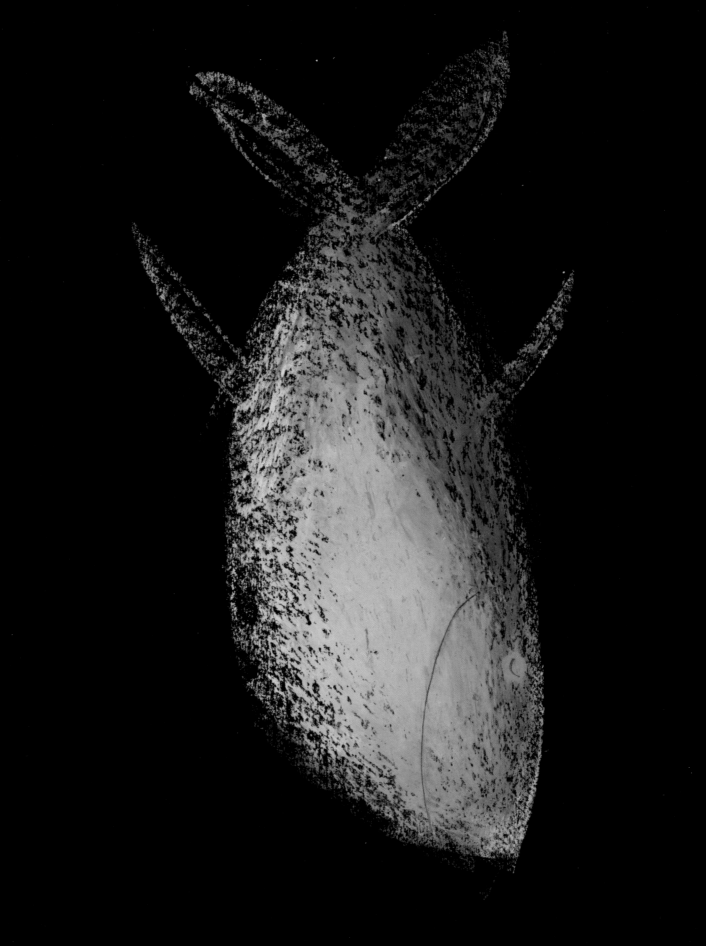